Cross Lines

Maeve Binchy

A Phoenix Paperback

This edition published in 1996 by Phoenix
a division of Orion Books Ltd
Orion House, 5 Upper St Martin's Lane, London WC2H 9EA

ISBN 1 85799 743 3

Typeset by Deltatype Ltd, Ellesmere Port, Cheshire
Printed in Great Britain by Clays Ltd, St Ives plc

CONTENTS

Cross Lines

Martin tapped his fingers in irritation on the phone. He was unsure of himself in his new and unfamiliar world of the Arts where he was heading. There were already too many stresses involved in this whole business without having to part from Angie in such an unsatisfactory way. Beautiful Angie, why hadn't she got up and pulled on a tracksuit? Why hadn't she said she'd drive him to the airport, they'd have coffee and a croissant together, it would have been so good. It would have calmed him down, to have sat with Angie, looking into her big dark eyes watching the passers-by envy him with this girl with the great mane of streaked hair and the big slow smile. He would have felt a million times more confident about the venture ahead. Instead of edgy and jumpy.

In the next booth he saw one of those kind of career women he disliked on sight. Short practical hair-do, mannish suit, enormous briefcase, immaculate make-up, gold watch pinned to a severe lapel. She was making a heavy statement about being equal and coping in a man's world. She was having a heated discussion with somebody on her telephone. Probably entirely unnecessary, shouting at someone for the sake of it. He would give Angie another three minutes and dial again. She had never been known to talk this long to anyone. And at nine thirty a.m.

Kay wished the man in the next phone box would stop staring at her, she had enough to cope with with one of Henry's tantrums. She had explained to Henry over and over how important it was for her to be at the trade fair a day in advance, that way she could supervise the setting up of the stand, make sure they had the right position, the one they had booked near the entrance, see that the lighting was adequate, decorate the booth, get to know the neighbours on her right and left so that she could rely on them and call on their support once the doors opened and the day's business began.

Henry had said he understood, but that was yesterday; today he was in one of his moods.

Kay would be gone for five days, she HATED leaving him like this, it was so uncalled for, he had nothing to fear from her trip to another town. She would be far too weary and exhausted to consider going out partying at the end of a long day, all she would want was a warm little telephone conversation every night, reassuring her that he loved her, that he was managing fine but not so fine as he managed when she was around and how he greatly looked forward to Friday. She had called him at the office to try and dispel his mood before it got a grip of him.

It had been a mistake, Henry's black disapproval came across the phone line loud and clear.

She had made her choice, she had decided for an extra day on this junket, and against going with him to his staff party. It was quite simple, she could take the consequences.

'What consequences?' Kay shouted, turning her back on the arty pseudo Bohemian in the next phone box.

He was handsome, she supposed, in that vain peacock way that a lot of actors or showbiz people adopt, mannered and self aware, stroking his cravat. The kind of man she most disliked. But it was increasingly hard to talk to Henry, the kind of man she most admired. He was showing none of those qualities that had marked him out when she met him first.

He pointed out that if Kay, his constant companion, was not going to bother to turn up at an important corporate gathering then he would regard himself as a single and unattached person with no commitments.

'That's blackmail of the worst kind.' Kay was appalled at herself for reacting like a teenager.

'The solution is in your hands', Henry said coldly. 'Come back from the airport now and we will forget the whole incident.' She hung up immediately, not trusting herself to speak to him.

Martin told himself that Angie's deep sleep was always important to her, she was a model, her face had to be unlined, untired at all times. She must have taken the telephone off the hook. His brow cleared when he remembered this, only to darken again when he remembered that as he kissed her goodbye he had said he would call from the airport and she had said that would be super. Why then, had she cut off his way of getting through to her?

Lost in their thoughts, neither Martin nor Kay realised that they had in fact been seated beside each other on the plane ... They looked at each other without pleasure. Martin took out the long complicated report on Arts funding which he was going to have to explain to various theatrical and artistic organisations, all of which were going to brand him as a cultural philistine. Kay read a report on last year's trade fair, and noted all the opportunities missed, contacts lost and areas of dissatisfaction. Their elbows touched lightly.

But they were unaware of each other. From time to time they lifted their eyes from the small print in their folders and Martin thought of all the times HE had driven Angie to her modelling assignments and Kay remembered all the corporate functions in HER firm that Henry had refused to attend without even the flimsiest excuse.

Above the clouds it was a lovely day, bright and clear. Kay felt her shoulders relaxing, and some of the tension leaving her. They were far above the complications and bustle of everything they had left behind: buildings, traffic, rush, corporate functions. She breathed deeply. She wished they could stay up here forever.

At that moment Martin sighed too, and with the first sign of a pleasant expression that he had shown, he said that it was a pity they couldn't stay up here forever.

'I was just thinking that. At exactly this moment,' Kay said, startled.

They talked easily, he of the problems ahead trying to convince earnest idealistic artists that he was not the voice of authority spelling out doom for their projects. He had been trying to dress like arty people as he knew that otherwise he would be dismissed as a Man in a Suit, which was apparently marginally better than being a child molester.

She told him of the poor results the company had achieved at last year's promotion, and how this was her first year in charge. There were many in the organisation who hoped she would fail and she feared they would be proved right. She knew that people thought she had got the post through some kind of feminine charm; she was dressing as severely as she could to show them that she wasn't flighty.

They were sympathetic and understanding. Martin told her what Henry never had, that perhaps she was over compensating, making herself look too stern and forbidding, killing off the good vibes she might otherwise have given.

Kay told Martin something that Angie had never thought

of – that possibly the cravat might be over the top. There was the possibility that the disaffected artistic folk might think he was playing a role.

They fell into companionable silence in the clear empty blue sky. And Martin thought that Angie probably didn't care about him at all, she cared only about her face, the magazine covers she appeared on and what bookings her agent might have for her next week. He would call her when they landed, a cheerful call, no accusations about taking the phone off the hook, she would wish him well, he would take the whole thing much more lightly from now on.

Kay wondered would Henry seriously take up with someone else as he had threatened. And would she mind very much if he did. She decided she would ring Henry's secretary and say how sorry she was to miss this evening's function, she would wish it well and say that sadly work had taken precedence. She would ask that Henry not be disturbed but insist that her message of goodwill was passed to those in the right places. This was a professional businesslike approach, not a very loving one. But Kay didn't feel very loving any more.

Then just at the same moment she and Martin left their private thoughts and turned to each other to talk again. Angie wasn't mentioned, nor was Henry, but strategy was, and optimism was exchanged.

Kay encouraged Martin to be straight with the groups, to tell them the worst news about funding first and try to work back into a position they felt was marginally more cheerful. Martin advised Kay to let her colleagues in on her hopes for their joint success, let them think they were creating it too. By the time they left the plane they were friends in everything but name. Martin considered asking her name but thought it might sound patronising. Kay wondered about giving him her card but feared it would look stereotype female executive.

There was a bank of telephones facing them in Arrivals. They both headed towards them.

Kay paused with her hand on the receiver. In the next box she saw Martin's fingers, not drumming this time but hesitating. Through the transparent walls they smiled at each other.

He looked less affected she thought, the velvet jacket's fine really.

She is quite elegant in spite of all that power dressing, he realised.

Neither of them made the phone call.

But it was too soon for any sudden decisions. There was work to be done. If they met each other somewhere again, well and good.

They wished each other luck and got into separate taxis.

As they settled back into their separate seats they each gave their taxi driver the name of the same hotel.

Package Tour

They met at a Christmas party and suddenly everything looked bright and full of glitter instead of commercial and tawdry as it had looked some minutes before.

They had got on like a house on fire and afterwards when they talked about it they wondered about the silly expression, a house on fire. It really didn't mean anything, like two people getting to know each other and discovering more and more things in common. They were the same age, each of them one quarter of a century old. Shane worked in a bank, Moya worked in an insurance office. Shane was from Galway and went home every month. Moya was from Clare and went home every three weeks. Shane's mother was difficult and wanted him to be a priest. Moya's father was difficult and had to be told that she was staying in a hostel in Dublin rather than a bedsitter.

Shane played a lot of squash because he was afraid of getting a heart attack or, worse, of getting fat and being passed over when aggressive lean fellows were promoted. Moya went to a gym twice a week because she wanted to look like Jane Fonda when she grew old and because she wanted to have great stamina for her holidays.

They both loved foreign holidays, and on their first evening out together, Shane told all about his trips to Tunisia, and Yugoslavia and Sicily. In turn Moya told her tales of Tangiers, Turkey and of Cyprus. Alone amongst their friends they seemed to think that a good foreign holiday was the high-spot of the year.

Moya said that most people she knew spent the money on clothes, and Shane complained that in his group it went on cars or drink. They were soul mates who had met over warm sparkling wine at a Christmas party where neither of them knew anyone else. It had been written for them in the stars.

When the January brochures came out, Moya and Shane were the first to collect them; they had plastic bags full of them before anyone else had got round to thinking of a holiday. They noted which were the bargains, where were early season or late season three-for-the-price-of-two-week holidays. They worked out the jargon.

Attractive flowers cascading down from galleries could mean the place was alive with mosquitoes. Panoramic views of the harbour might mean the hotel was up an unmerciful hill. Simple might mean no plumbing and sophisticated could suggest all-night discos.

The thing they felt most bitter about was the Single Room Supplement. It was outrageous to penalise people for being individuals. *Why* should travel companies expect that people go off on their holidays two by two like the animals into an ark? And how was it that the general public obeyed them so slavishly? Moya could tell you of people who went on trips with others simply on the basis that they all got their holidays in the first fortnight in June.

Shane said that he knew fellows who went to Spain as friends and came home as enemies because their outing had been on the very same basis. Timing.

But as the months went on and the meetings became more frequent and the choice of holiday that each of them would settle for was gradually narrowed down they began to realise that this summer they would probably travel together. That it was silly to put off this realisation. They had better admit it.

They admitted it easily one evening over a plate of spaghetti.

It had been down to two choices now. The Italian lakes or the island of Crete. And somehow it came to both of them at the same time; this would be the year they would go to Crete. The only knotty problem was the matter of the Single Room.

They were not as yet lovers. They didn't want to be rushed into it by the expediency of a double booking. They didn't want it to be put off limits by the fact of having booked two separate rooms. Shane said that perhaps the most sensible thing would be to book a room with two beds. This had to be stipulated on the booking form. A twin bedded room. Not a double bed.

Shane and Moya assured each other they were grown-ups. They could sleep easily in two separate beds, and suppose in the fullness of time, after mature consideration and based on an equal decision with no one party forcing the other . . . they wanted to sleep in the same bed . . . then the facility, however narrow, would be there for them.

They congratulated each other on their maturity and paid the booking deposit. They had agreed on a middle of the road kind of hotel, in one of the resorts that had not yet been totally discovered and destroyed. They had picked June, which they thought would avoid the worst crowds, they each had a savings plan. They knew that this year was going to be the best year in their lives and the holiday would be the first of many taken together all over the world.

The cloud didn't come over the horizon until March, when they were sitting companionably reading a glossy magazine. Shane pointed out a huge suitcase on wheels with a matching smaller suitcase. Weren't they smashing, he said; a bit pricey but maybe it would be worth it.

Moya thought she must be looking at the wrong page. Those were the kind of suitcases that Americans bought for going round the world.

Shane thought that Moya couldn't be looking at the right page, they were just two normal suitcases, but smart and easy to identify on the carousel. Just right for a two-week holiday. But for how many people, Moya wondered wildly; 11

surely the two of them wouldn't have enough to fill even the smaller suitcase. Well for one person, me, Shane said with a puzzled look.

Between the two happy young people there was a sudden grey area. Up to now their relationship had been so open and free, but suddenly there were unspoken things hovering in the air. They had told each other that their friends' romances had failed and even their marriages had rocked because they had never been able to clear the air. Shane and Moya would not be like that. But still neither one of them seemed able to bring up the subject of the suitcase. The gulf between them was huge.

Yet in other ways they seemed just as happy as before: they went for walks along the pier, they played their squash and went to the gym, they enjoyed each other's friends, and both of them managed to put the disturbing black cloud about the luggage into the background of their minds. Until April, when another storm came and settled on them.

It was Moya's birthday and she unwrapped her gift from Shane, which was a travelling iron. She turned it round and round and examined it in case it was something else disguised as a travelling iron. In the *hope* that it was something disguised as a travelling iron. But no, that's what it was.

It was lovely, she said faintly.

Shane said he knew ladies loved to have something to take the creases out on holidays, and perhaps Moya shouldn't throw away the tissue paper, it was terrific for folding into clothes when you were packing, it took out all that crumpled look, didn't she find?

Moya sat down very suddenly. Absolutely on a different subject she said she wondered how many shirts Shane took on holiday. Well fifteen obviously, and the one he was wearing and sports shirts and a couple of beach shirts.

'Twenty shirts?' Moya said faintly.

That was about it.

And would there be twenty socks and knickers too? Well, give or take. Give or take how many? A pair or two. There seemed to be a selection of shoes and belts, and the odd sunhat.

Moya felt all the time that Shane would smile his lovely familiar heart-turning smile and say 'I had you fooled hadn't I?' and they would fall happily into each other's arms. But Shane said nothing.

Shane was hoping that Moya would tell him soon where all this list of faintly haranguing questions was leading. Why she was asking him in such a dalek voice about perfectly normal things? It was as if she asked him did he brush his teeth or did he put on his clothes before leaving the house. He stared at her anxiously. Perhaps he wasn't showing enough interest in her wardrobe? Maybe he should ask about her gear.

That did not seem to be a happy solution. Moya, it turned out, was a person who had never checked in a suitcase in her life, she had a soft squelchy bag of the exact proportions that would fit under an airline seat and would pass as Carry on Baggage. She brought three knickers, three bras, three shirts, three skirts and three bathing suits. She brought a sponge bag, a pair of flip-flop sandals and a small tube of travel detergent.

She thought that a holiday should never involve waiting for your bags at any airport, and never take in dressing for dinner, and the idea of carrying home laundry bags of dirty clothes was as foreign to her as it was to Shane that anyone would spend holiday time washing things and drying them.

'But it takes no time at all if you bring spares,' pleaded Shane. 'The arms would come out of your sockets carrying that lot,' said Moya. 'We wouldn't get into the bathroom with all your clothes draped round it,' said Shane.

They talked about it very reasonably as they had always promised each other they would do. But the rainbows had gone, and the glitter had dimmed.

It would have been better if they had actually met on holidays they said, with Moya carrying the shabby holdall and Shane the handsome and excessive luggage. Then they would have known from the start that they weren't people who had the same views about a package tour and how you packed for it. It was a hurdle they might have crossed before they fell in love. Not a horrible shock at the height of romance.

14   They were practical, Moya and Shane; they wondered

would it iron itself out if they paid the Single Room Supplement. That way Moya wouldn't see the offending Sultan's Wardrobe as she kept calling it, and Shane wouldn't be blinded by wet underwear as he kept fearing. But no, it went deeper than that. It seemed to show the kind of people they were; too vastly different ever to spend two weeks, let alone a lifetime together.

As the good practical friends they were, they went back to the travel agency and transferred their bookings to separate holidays with separate hopes and dreams.

The Consultant Aunt

Mother had been the eldest of her family and Aunt Miriam the youngest, so Miriam was more like a cousin than an aunt. Miriam worked with management consultants. Sarah had always been fascinated by the stories of how they got to the root of the problem here, spotted the trouble there, cut out the dead wood somewhere else. Miriam must live a very exciting life, Sarah had always thought. Compared to everyone around her, it was positively star quality.

Mother always sighed when she spoke of Miriam. 'Thinks she knows everything, that's always been her problem,' she said. Sometimes she said it to Miriam's face. 'You're too definite, dear, that's your weakness. Men don't like women with such very forthright views.'

'Oh, I think they do,' Miriam said.

'Well you haven't shown any proof of it,' Mother sniffed.

'Oh, by not being *married*, is that what you mean?'

'Don't get me wrong dear, you're very attractive, much the best looking in our family, but how was it that the rest of us were all well married by your age?'

'I don't know.' Miriam pretended to consider it seriously. 'It's a mystery.'

Sarah loved it when Miriam came to supper, and even more when she came for the weekend. Sarah was doing A levels. Nobody else seemed to understand what it felt like. The feeling that you were too old for all this kind of study, that it was taking time from important things like the disco, and Simon who told Sarah he liked her but he wouldn't wait for ever.

Miriam would lie on Sarah's bed as if she were seventeen also instead of twenty-five. She never nagged Sarah about getting on with her work: she talked about Simon as if he were a real person instead of throwing her eyes up to heaven about him as Mother did, or sighing heavily like Father.

'Why does he threaten, do you think?' Miriam asked about Simon. 'Do you think it's because he's mad about you, or could it mean there's a bullying streak in him?'

For ages they would discuss it, and then Sarah always ended up, 'What do *you* think Miriam? What would you do?'

Each time Miriam was firm. 'I'm hundreds of years older than you are, surely you don't want *my* advice.'

But Sarah always did, and it always worked like a dream. She told Simon that year that she would be very happy to go out with him on Friday evenings but at no other time because she wanted to study. She would go out with no other boy and he could consider them going steady just as 17 long as he realised that she literally would not leave her books.

Simon said he thought that was perfectly fair, and that he would concentrate on his work – he had a job in a big hi-fi and stereo store. When it came to July, Simon had been promoted within the chain, had saved enough for a small car, and Sarah had done well in her A levels.

Simon was twenty. Two years older than her. He said he'd like to get married when he was twenty-one.

Sarah lay on the bed this time, and Miriam sat in the chair listening. Simon had been so good to her, had accepted all the restrictions she laid down. He had agreed not to discuss sleeping with her until the A levels were over. Now they were, he was discussing it pretty regularly, and talking about marriage at the same time.

'Well would you *like* to make love with him?' Miriam made it sound as if it was a thing you could do or needn't do.

'I don't know.'

'Well you don't have to until you do know. I mean, it's not a thing you do because you think someone's been kind to you and might expect it. The postman's jolly kind here, and I'm sure he thinks you're very attractive, but you don't have to make agonising decisions about yes or no with him, do you?'

Things were always beautifully simple with Miriam. You described what you wanted and then you went ahead and did it. Miriam said it was all like management consultancy.

The biggest thing was identifying the problem. Once you had done that, then it was quite easy to solve it.

Miriam was small and dark, with lots of dark brown hair which she wore in a thick shiny bob. Miriam believed in consulting the best. She had gone once to a very expensive hairdresser and asked his advice. What hairstyle would be the most flattering? She took his advice and said she would go back to him every three years. He had laughed and said that his business would fall apart like a house of cards if everyone was as practical as Miriam. But then he was fortunate; the world was filled with consultant Aunts who knew exactly what they wanted and how to get it.

Sarah explained to Simon that she didn't want to get into a relationship yet. She wanted to think about her career. Simon was very annoyed. He called her a tease.

Miriam curled up on the window seat and listened to the sad saga.

'I honestly don't know what he's complaining about. As a result of you, he's saved his money, he's got promotion, he had you as a date every Friday. It's not as if you took everything and gave nothing. No, he's got it all wrong.' With Miriam it was all so clear.

Sarah gave an exact parrot version of her aunt's speech. To her surprise, it worked. Simon said that was indeed true, he had been highly unreasonable. He agreed they should be friends, pals, mates, they would go out together when it suited them, they would have other friends or no other friends as they thought fit. Simon believed he had reached these dizzying heights of maturity on his own. By Christmas he told Sarah that he had found another girl, and she *did* want to get married. So if there were no hard feelings . . .

There were no hard feelings. Sarah even brought a Christmas present for his fiancée over to Simon's house.

The fiancée, a silly giggling girl, said she would never be able to live up to Sarah, she said that Simon's first love had been a star.

'Do you think I'll be a spinster sort of a star?' Sarah asked Miriam in a troubled tone. 'I mean, I don't want to have very high principles and be thought magnificent but live my life on my own, enviously watching young lovers holding hands.'

Miriam pealed with laughter. 'A beautiful eighteen-year-old girl on the brink of life, and you talk like that! Look at me, I'm twenty-six. I've not exactly held back on relationships; I don't look like an Old Maid sitting primly on a shelf watching the lovers of the world go by two by two, now do I?'

Sarah agreed. Even though Mother said it wasn't natural for Miriam to prowl the world in that expensive outfit and that glossy hair-do. She should have settled down like everyone else.

Christmas was always much more fun when Miriam came: she simply loved hearing about their problems and trying to solve them. She would take notes about Father's company, and ask him dozens of questions, and then triumphantly come up with the solution: they should give up their own transport, they didn't need a fleet of vans and lorries which took up so much time and were not at all cost-effective, instead they should have a rental agreement. It worked, and Father was the hero of the firm. It was the same with Sarah's brother Jack and the problems in the club. In their case, Miriam worked out, the difficulties arose from not having proper permanent premises of their own, which they could then let out and use to earn revenue. Jack was made President for his far-seeing views.

And Mother had groaned and complained about the kitchen. It really wasn't practical, it wasn't big enough to eat in, yet it was wearying carrying everything through to the other room. It was Miriam who saw that if you had a long hatch between the two rooms it would give everyone more light, provide a place for books and the record player as well as a shelf for passing things through.

'There would be cooking smells,' complained Mother.

'A fan,' said Miriam.

'Suppose we wanted to keep the sitting room private for some reason?' Mother protested.

'Why? Do you make love on the floor in there or something?'

When the alterations were finished Mother draped the shelves in houseplants and trailing ivy, and received the compliments of all her friends with a lofty air.

For Sarah, Miriam was her consultant Aunt about everything; clothes, career, but mainly life and love.

The career was easy. Miriam recommended Sarah to apply to a firm which took bright young management trainees. Soon she was on the ladder there, well in control of her work.

When Sarah was twenty-one, Miriam pointed out the advantage of getting a mortage and buying a small flat. Sarah didn't want to live at home under the parental eye for ever.

'I might as well, considering that I live like a nun,' Sarah wailed.

Miriam was now an elegant twenty-nine: her hair was a mass of bubbly black curls: she looked smarter than ever. 'It sounds to me as if you are ready to have a relationship,' the consultant Aunt said firmly.

'Find me someone, Miriam,' Sarah begged in mock helplessness.

'No, certainly not. But in the middle of negotiating loans and getting the flat, someone's bound to turn up. Wiser not to find anyone at work, I always think.' Miriam's dark eyes twinkled, with some memories, possibly. Sarah agreed.

Through Miriam she found the perfect flat, the right mortgage, the exact furniture, the out-of-work art student to paint the place for her, and Peter. Peter was the solicitor, thirtyish, blond, very handsome and very anxious to settle down. Sarah fell hopelessly in love with him.

That was exactly what it was, she told Miriam on the first Christmas after she had left home: hopeless. There was no hope that bachelor Peter would make a move, he was set in his independent ways.

They had gone to Sarah's family home; Miriam had pointed out that Sarah's mother would have nothing to think about all autumn if the prospect of a family Christmas was denied her. They sat as usual in Sarah's old bedroom solving the problems of the world.

'This is one you *can't* solve,' Sarah said sadly. 'You can't make him love me and want me for ever.'

'Like hell I can't,' Miriam cried, the light of battle in her eyes.

It was the most exciting campaign she had ever fought. Sarah had to follow it exactly, every step. Otherwise it would fail.

The seduction was planned for New Year's Eve. Sarah was to invite him to her friend's glittery party.

'What friend?' Sarah asked innocently.

'Your friend Miriam, idiot,' Miriam said.

The guest list was picked so that Peter would like the people there. Something would happen so that his car wouldn't start afterwards. Miriam was very sound on mechanical things. So Peter and Sarah would have to stay the night, for who could get a garage or a taxi on New Year's Eve? Miriam's house was large, and she would employ a waiter for the night so that when they woke next morning the place would not look like a pigsty. She would disappear, leaving a note about orange juice and champagne in the fridge.

It worked like a dream, exactly as Miriam had predicted. Peter was very straight and said that he hoped he hadn't taken advantage of Sarah and he didn't want any permanent commitment. She agreed utterly, it was the last thing on her mind.

They continued to visit each other's flats all that winter. Miriam taught Sarah how to make instant gourmet meals for him without any of the mumsy flour-covered scenario which drove bachelors spare. Without appearing to take over his life, Sarah, under Miriam's minutely detailed instructions, did so.

Peter found that his laundry was always perfect these days, not because Sarah did his washing – Miriam would have a blue fit over such domesticity – but instead Sarah arranged for a laundry service to pick it up and return it at convenient times and to send their account to Peter monthly. When Sarah wasn't around the service didn't arrive, because Peter didn't know how to organise it. He was always delighted to see Sarah back from her business trips.

Miriam said that she should organise some social life for Peter who, though highly successful in his office, was like many men utterly unable to get his act together at home. Again with meticulous instruction, Sarah arranged little drinks parties, little theatre outings, little picnics.

By autumn he couldn't live without her. And he told her so. Miriam had advised playing a little hard to get, pretending that she didn't wish to be tied down.

'But I'll lose him,' Sarah wailed.

'No you won't, he'll want you more than ever. Believe me, I've studied the market, I know what's out there.'

She was right.

Peter bought a ring at Christmas: he wanted to come and ask her father's approval. And this was the man who one year back had been busy explaining that he didn't want to get involved. Somehow, it seemed too easy to Sarah.

At Christmas time in her old bedroom, she and Miriam talked it through again. Miriam was an elegant thirty. Again, it was impossible to imagine her looking better. She listened sympathetically.

'I think you've outgrown him,' she said eventually.

That was exactly what Sarah had done. It had been too simple and somehow unsatisfactory to win a man by ploys. It had nothing to do with love and trust and wanting to share a life. Sarah was very despondent.

'It might just mean he's not the right one, there are others,' Miriam said.

Sarah was thoughtful. 'Is this what happened to you, Miriam, that you were so smart you didn't want them in the end because you had won them too easily?'

'No, I don't think so. If it was the right one, it wouldn't 25 matter *how* you won him,' Miriam said.

Peter was astounded. There was no way that Sarah could explain it to him, each attempt was less satisfactory than the one before it.

They parted amicably.

'You're too ambitious, you think only of your work,' he said when they had their last dinner. It was very civilised. She had brought him back his records, and his books, two chunky sweaters and an alarm clock that played 'Land of Hope and Glory'. She had collected her own things without drama, and they were already in the boot of the car. She realised that he didn't even know how to work the dishwasher she had made him buy, but she hardened her heart. He would learn, there was a book of instructions.

'I don't think only of my work,' she said, and looked at his soft fair hair and kind face. He would have made a good father to their children. But she had got him too easily. She could have betrayed him as easily.

'But I will concentrate on work,' she added as an afterthought. 'I will spend two or three years thinking of little else.'

Miriam hardly needed to help her rise and rise in the firm. And she learned about power dressing, and how under no circumstances must any woman at a meeting ever pour the coffee or clear up the cups. When Sarah was twenty-five, she was a woman to be reckoned with.

Miriam at thirty-three looked dazzling. Her hair was

now a wonderful red. She was a full partner and director in the company. She had been written about in magazines and interviewed for the Sunday papers.

Sarah met Miriam's partner Robert at the office Christmas party. Miriam's office parties were splendid – no paper cups, no silly gropings over too much vodka, it had all been planned months in advance but seemed utterly casual. Smoked salmon and scrambled eggs, lots of good brown bread was served. It turned out to be what everyone thought they needed.

'Isn't Miriam quite wonderful?' Sarah said, turning to Robert, and as she spoke she felt something extraordinary happen inside her chest, possibly near her heart; she felt something slip out of place like a zip fastener opening or a strap breaking. She caught her breath but the feeling would not go away. As she looked into the dark blue eyes of Robert Gray, the senior partner and managing director of Miriam's company, she knew she had fallen ridiculously in love.

They talked about it at Christmas.

'His wife?' Sarah asked tremulously.

'What about her?' Miriam asked.

'Is she . . . I mean, I don't want to . . . perhaps she's quite awful and doesn't love him. Perhaps?' She looked pleadingly at Miriam.

Miriam shook her head. 'We've never won anything by refusing to face facts. Susie is quite lovely in every way, she 27 is charming, good fun, great company, a devoted mother and wife, and she adores Robert.'

'Well that's it,' Sarah said, tears of shock and rage coming to her eyes.

'Not neccessarily,' said Miriam. And they sat and talked as they had so often sat and talked in this room, while the sound of Christmas carols came up from the record player.

It was a busy three months. And Sarah hated a lot of it. She hated the visit to Robert and Susie's home. She felt almost sick when Susie asked her to leave her coat in the bedroom, and she saw the big bed with its patchwork quilt and lovely curtains. This room would be a different place at the end of the year. Would Susie Gray sit here and wonder where she had gone wrong, and why it had to happen this way? But Miriam had always said don't go into it unless you're going to go the distance.

Sarah had hesitated, especially after visiting their home.

'Well decide,' Miriam was brisk. 'If it's no, then we drop it now, you get back into mainstream work, we find you someone else, you buy a budgie and start knitting. But if you want him, Sarah, then let's go get him.'

Three months after she had met him at that Christmas office party, Sarah was sitting in a small romantic restaurant with Robert Gray. There had been a series of meetings in offices and business lunches before this, of course, on a series of excuses dreamed up by Miriam. Then they needed to talk for longer and more privately about a company matter.

'I'd ask you home, but there are children and wives running all over the place,' he smiled.

'I'd ask you home too, but we might be misunderstood, let's keep it neutral in a restaurant,' Sarah replied. And with Miriam's help, found the most impossibly attractive place with quiet tables, lots of flowers and discreet music.

By summer they were lovers.

By autumn he said he couldn't live without her, but that he could not leave his wife. Under heavy coaching, Sarah said of course he mustn't dream of leaving Susie and the children. She forced herself to take business trips, to go on a holiday, to take a week in a health farm.

It worked wonders. By winter he wanted her so desperately he said he would do anything.

Miriam said she should strike in the new year, demand a 'Susie or me' situation.

'It's so hard to hurt someone good and trusting like that.' Sarah still felt guilty.

'What do we do in business every day except take advantage of people more trusting and simple than we are? If we paused every moment, where would we be today?'

It was a fact.

At Christmas they sat in Sarah's old room. Miriam seemed feverish with excitement.

'You were quite right to say no phone calls, no letters, nothing at all. It will put him on his mettle. He will know he 29 can't play fast and loose with you.'

'Are you *sure*, Miriam? It seems so cold not to talk to him at all over Christmas, especially if we think he's making up his mind to leave her.'

'But this is *precisely* the right way to firm up his decision,' Miriam said. Her eyes were almost too bright. Sarah wondered was it healthy for her aunt to take such an interest in manipulating people's lives.

She stuck it out: no calls, no letters. She went back to her own comfortable flat just before New Year. He would have left letters, he would have left flowers, surely. There would be anguished messages on her answering machine.

There were no messages.

Sarah's heart gave several unexpected little jumps. She reached for the phone to call Miriam. There was no reply.

Nobody was working today. *Where* could Miriam be? She rang Robert's house just to hear his voice, she would hang up then.

Susie answered the phone, Her voice sounded choked, as if she had a cold, or as if she had been crying. Sarah hung up.

She went around to Miriam's flat. It had an empty look about it. That was odd: Miriam had come back here yesterday, she should be there.

She called Miriam's neighbour, a kind old man who often took in parcels when Miriam was not at home.

'Went off to the sun, she did. Three weeks. Oh, she's a lucky woman, is Miriam.'

To the *sun*! It was beyond belief.

'And he was a nice man that came to fetch her. I've seen him with her, of course, but I thought he was just a business partner.'

Sarah phoned Susie again. It was not a cold, she had been crying.

Sarah went around to the house. It had been like a bolt from the blue, Susie said.

Sarah went to her office. She let herself in with her master key. As she had expected, the notes were there.

Robert wrote that he could not believe how cold she had been, how unloving and dismissive when he had been prepared to dismantle his marriage for her, when he had in fact destroyed his marriage, and then to find this heartless and inexplicable staying out of touch. He would make a new life, but first he would have a holiday. He had got these tickets for the West Indies, he was sorry things had turned out as they had, he would always remember the good times.

The note from her aunt was shorter. It was the kind of note that could have been shown in a court of law without revealing anything. It said that in business you always had to take advantage of those more trusting and simple than you. It said that unless you were prepared to go the distance there was no point in starting the journey.

It wished Sarah well for the New Year.

The Apprenticeship

It was to be one of the most stylish weddngs of the year. Florrie thought that if anyone had been giving odds a quarter of a century ago when she was born whether this child would ever be a guest at something like this, those odds would have been enormous. A child born in a small house in a small street in Wigan didn't seem likely to end up as the bride's best friend at what the newspapers were calling the wedding of the decade. If only her mother had lived, Florrie thought, if only her father had cared. They might have been able to get some mileage out of it, some reward for the long hours of work, the high hopes.

There would be pictures of Florrie in tomorrow's papers, probably a glimpse of her on tonight's television news. She would figure certainly in the glossy magazines, her hat alone would ensure she was well snapped. She would be seen laughing and sharing a joke probably with some youngish and handsome member of the aristocracy. This would not be hard, because unusually for a society wedding there might not be many young women friends of the bride around. And the groom's friends, being horsey, would not be as photogenic. No, Florrie knew that she would figure in the *Tatler* and *Harper's*. And she knew how to smile without showing a mouthful of teeth and how to raise her chin which made her neck look long and upper class. She knew that it looked much more classy not to be seen with a glass in her hand, but to appear fascinated by the particular braying chap that she was meant to be talking to.

Florrie knew all of this because she had worked at it, and learned it. Like she had never worked at anything when she was at school. Long ago in a different place and at a different time, with Camilla, except of course that Camilla had not been Camilla then, she had been Ruby. And Ruby and Florrie had been best friends. As in many ways they were still best friends today. The society columns might well describe Florrie tomorrow as a very close friend of the bride. But they would not say that they had grown up together, that they had shared great doorstep sandwiches in their lunch hour, that they had collected old newspapers just so that they could read the society pages and see how people lived in a different and better world.

They had read their subject carefully, young Ruby and young Florrie. No hint of social climbing or being a hanger-on. Not even the most suspicious could fault Camilla or catch her out in a lie today. Camilla had always said she was from way up North, that her parents were dead, that she had hardly any family. Better to stick as close to the truth as possible, she had advised Florrie, less for them to unearth, 33 and you can never be caught out in a lie. Even if they found out she had once been Ruby, Camilla was prepared to say it had been a pet name. She thought it was terribly brave and funny of Florrie to hold on to her name. But then Florrie was such a character! Florrie had held on to her name because she remembered her mother holding her as a little girl.

'I had a doll once called Florrie,' her mother had said. 'I never thought I'd have a little baby of my own, a beautiful baby to look after.' Florrie was three when she heard this first, hardly a baby, and still further from babyhood when her mother dressed her for school and held her face gently between red rough hands. 'Florrie,' she had breathed in a voice full of admiration and love. 'Such a beautiful name for a beautiful little girl. They wanted me to call you Caroline . . . but I wanted a beautiful name for you, one you'd love . . . Florence. It means a flower, little Florrie, beautiful little flower.'

Ruby's mother might have thought she was a little jewel. She might even have said so, but Camilla never said it. Camilla said nothing about her parents. Except that they were dead. Which was true.

They had died together in a coach crash, on the very first holiday of their married life. Florrie's father had said that's what you got for grand ideas, coach tours to the Continent, no less. Florrie's mother had said maybe they should take in the child. Ruby was eleven, she had nobody else. Everyone had said it was a great idea. After all, it was unusual to be an only child in their street. Now Ruby and Florrie were like twins. And apart from reading all those 'silly books' as people called the magazines they read, they were sensible girls too. Not silly like some, not getting into trouble with boys. Hard working. On Saturdays they worked in the beauty salon, and they learned how it was all done. The proprietor never had two such willing assistants. As well as sweeping floors and folding towels, they stood entranced watching the facials, and manicures.

The customers liked them, two bright youngsters full of unqualified admiration. The customers didn't know they had come to learn. As they went to the fashion stores to learn, and as they worked in the good hotel to watch. And they did secretarial courses at night. By the time they had their 'O' levels they were ready for anything. Ruby was ready to leave, to go South to start Stage Two. Florrie could go nowhere, her mother was failing fast.

She sat by her mother's bed and listened to the homespun wisdom, with a heart that was filled with impatience as well as love. She heard her mother beg her to believe that Dad was a good man really. It was just that he was a bit mulish, and drank a little too much. Dad had said no kind word in the seventeen years that Florrie had lived in his house. She nodded and pretended that she agreed with the mother who would not be leaving hospital and coming home. Her mother said that Ruby was right to have gone to London, 35 she was impatient, she would have been silly to stay around. The woman found nothing odd that the child she had taken in had abandoned her. Ruby has great unhappiness in her soul, she said. Florrie sat by the bed and gritted her teeth. Patience and forgiveness like this were unrealistic. Surely they couldn't be considered virtues. The nurses liked her, the handsome tall girl, a blonde with well-cut hair and long pink fingernails, unlike her stooped and work-weary mother. The daughter had character, the nurses told each other. She wouldn't stay long with the bad-tempered father once the poor woman passed away.

Florrie stayed a week. Her father's farewell was grudging, as every other gesture had been. He had always known she would go, he said, too high and mighty by far for them. No, she needn't keep coming back up, there wasn't all that much more to say.

Florrie was astonished at the change in her friend in ten short months. Vowel sounds had altered, and that wasn't all. Ruby was no longer Ruby. It's only a name, she had explained, it could have been anything.

'I know,' Florrie had said. 'I should have been Caroline.'

'Then *be* Caroline,' Camilla had begged.

'Never.' Florrie's eyes had flashed at the thought.

They looked at each other then, a long look.

'It's only the name,' Florrie had said eventually. 'I'm on for everything else.'

And it was like the old days, they laughed as they heard

each other's phrases, you never said you had been to the WC or the toilet, it was the lavatory. You didn't say serviette, you said napkin, and it wasn't posh to have paper ones that you could throw away when they got crumpled. They had plenty of time, it was an apprenticeship, they told each other. They had until they were twenty, then they would be ready. To move among the smart and the beautiful, to be at ease among them, to marry them and live in comfort for the rest of their lives.

It would only be hard if they were unprepared. They had heard too many tales of people being trapped by their humble origins. Camilla and Florrie would be different. They would invent no pedigree which could be checked and found faulty. They would shrug and ask did such things matter any more. They would look so much the part and seem to care so little about proving themselves that soon they would be accepted. They would try hard but would never be seen to try at all, that was the secret.

And soon they were indeed ready. And it wasn't nearly as difficult as they thought. There was a career structure. Chalet girls in ski resorts, a few weeks working in smart jewellers and in art houses so that they met the right type of girl. They were slow to take up with the right type of men at the beginning. They wanted other girls to be their allies at the start. And anyway, they wanted to be ready when they found the really right men. They had noticed that it wasn't only the Royals who liked their girlfriends not to have played the field, a lot of the Uppers thought that girls who had been around a lot might not be good wife material, and after all one wouldn't like to think that lots of chaps had been with one's wife, what?

And in the meantime, because they *were* so bright and met so many people, they actually got good jobs. Camilla was high up in an estate agency and Florrie was now a partner in a firm of interior decorators. Years of watching for quality and trying to define it had paid off for both of them.

And then Camilla showed a couple of town houses to a chap who thought she was quite super and asked her to his place in the country for the weekend. She went, but she was slower than he thought to begin with a teeny affair, as he called it. In fact she was adamant about not beginning it. He complained about her bitterly over a bottle of Bollinger to his friend. Albert. Albert said that it was very rum, the girl must be mad. He'd like to meet her, he always liked meeting mad people.

Albert was of blood so blue that it almost frightened Camilla off. But she decided to take him on. This was the challenge she had spent years rehearsing for. This was the prize she had hardly dared to hope for.

Albert was intrigued by her. The girl who hadn't been to bed with his friend, who wouldn't go to bed with him either. Who wasn't frightened of his mother, who was 38 casual to the point of indifference about her own background. She was not a gold-digger, she had a position of importance in her firm. Nobody could see the potential like Camilla, they said. She dressed well, she seemed to have lots of girl-friends who all spoke glowingly of her. She had no past.

Camilla played it beautifully, she waited until Albert was truly besotted and at that precise moment she told him she was thinking of moving to Washington DC. There had been interest and offers, she was vague lest he ask her what interest and which offers. But she had timed it right. Albert couldn't let her leave. Albert's father predictably said she was a fine-looking filly but had she any breeding, his mother unpredictably said she was about the only kind of woman who might make a success of Albert and the rolling acres, and the complicated property investments and the tied cottages. The wedding of the decade was on.

It was decided between them that Florrie should not be the bridesmaid, the press would be too inquisitive, would ask about their origins. Papers nowadays did horrible things. They might send a photographer up to that small street and, perish the thought, find Florrie's father, surly in his braces. And he might tell that Camilla was Ruby and that her parents had been killed on their first coach tour abroad.

Better to have six flower girls and Albert's horsey-looking sister. Wiser to have the lovely Florrie stand out among the guests. A young woman of elegance, successful in her field. Further proof if any were needed that the bride was the right stuff, or as right as you can get in these days of social change and upheaval.

Florrie stood in the old church, and looked up at the flags of the regiment that Albert's family had fought in. The stained glass window remembered various ancestors, and the pews had brass plates recalling the family. The Bishop was old and genial. He spoke of duty and of hope. Florrie listened as she looked at Camilla's beautiful face; she knew that her friend was listening too.

Then the Bishop spoke of love. He told how it conquered everything and that it cast out envy and ambition and greed. His eyes became misty when he talked of love.

The night before, Florrie and Camilla had talked for a long time. They had talked as they had never been able to talk since that day when Florrie had come to London and said she would change everything, everything but her name. They laughed as they hadn't laughed for years, they drank champagne instead of the lemon tea which they had learnt to like when they were fourteen because they had read it was lower class to take milk.

They had said that the battle had been half won, and now that Camilla was in, she could have the right kind of dinner parties and house-parties to launch her friend. Her talented friend with the wonderfully funny name. They had embraced and congratulated each other on their magical

apprenticeship.

But they hadn't talked about love. And in the church where Albert's bones would lie one day, very probably beside the bones of her friend Ruby, Florrie shivered. She knew that as far as she was concerned the apprenticeship was over. She had got far enough. Perhaps she had got much farther than her friend, who would appear in tomorrow's papers as the bride of the decade, who would be called Lady Camilla, who would live a life without love. They said that young girls' heads were meant to be filled with stories of love but that had never happened to Ruby or Florrie. There had been no room in their heads, the space was too filled with rule books on how to behave and how to say glad to know you rather than pleased to meet you. It had been too busy an apprenticeship to allow for thoughts of love.

Florrie would make time for it, she thought. She would not list the likely guests that she might trap at her friend's long table, smiling at them confidently through Albert's family silver. When a bishop or vicar or a registrar came to say the word for Florrie, the word love wouldn't have an alien ring to it.

She felt somehow that the mother who had thought of her as a flower would have been pleased with her, and she was aware of tears beginning to well up in her eyes. But she willed them back, because the upper classes do not cry at christenings, weddings or funerals. It is after all what sets them apart. Her apprenticeship had not been wasted.

Excitement

Everyone said that Rose was immensely practical. She was attractive looking, of course, and always very well groomed. A marvellous wife for Denis, a wonderful mother for Andrew and Celia. And a gifted teacher. People said that Rose was a shining example. Or if they were feeling less generous, they said that they had never known anyone to fall on her feet like Rose. Married at twenty-five to a successful young man, two children, a boy and a girl, a job to stop her going mad in the house all day, her own car, her own salary every month, no husband grousing about the cost of highlights. Why wouldn't she be a shining example?

It had been Rose who suggested the whole idea of the Sunday brunches. They had all come from the tyranny of family lunches with great roasts and heavy midday meals. So they moved from house to house every Sunday, everyone bringing a bottle of wine and some kind of salad thing. They all dressed up. The children played together. If any couple wanted to bring along a friend they could.

They congratulated themselves, it kept them young and exciting they thought. Not dead and lumpen like their parents had been. And it had been Rose's idea in the first place.

Of course another example of Rose's luck was that her mother lived way down in Cork. She wasn't constantly on the doorstep criticising the way that the grandchildren were being brought up. Twice a year Rose's mother came to Dublin, twice a year Rose took the children to Cork. It was yet another example of how well she organised her life. So they would have been very surprised if they knew how discontented Rose felt as half term was approaching. She seemed to have been teaching for ever. The same things every year, and in the same words. Ony the faces in front of her were different, the younger sisters of the children she had already taught.

Then on the home front there would be the same arguments with Andrew, six, and Celia five, about which place to visit when they went to the zoo. Andrew wanted snakes and lions, Celia wanted birds and bunnies. And there would be the same discussions with the au pair. A different name every year, but always the same discussion – the time she came home at night, the long-distance phone calls. And Denis! Well, he was pretty much the same too. There would be the usual jokes about life being a holiday for teachers, about the workers of the world like himself having to toil on. In a million years he would never suggest the two of them went away together. It wouldn't matter what kind of a place. Even a simple guest house. But it wouldn't cross his mind. And if Rose were to suggest it, Denis would say he shouldn't really go away. Business was different from teaching, you had to stay in touch. And then what about Sunday? Surely Rose wouldn't want to miss their Sunday with all the gang. Rose began to wish she had never invented these Sundays. They were a lash for her back.

Always being bright and cheerful, always thinking up a different little dish to make them ooh and aah, blow-drying her hair, putting on make-up, reading the Sunday papers so as not to be out of the conversation, bribing Andrew and Celia to behave. It was always the same.

Rose was quiet as the time came up towards the half-term holiday. Nancy, her friend in the staff room, noticed. 'Where's all the zip and get up and go?' she asked. Nancy was single and always saying in mock despair that she would never find a man. 'A bit of the magic seems to be going from it all,' Rose said more truthfully and seriously than she had intended to. 'Maybe he has the seven-year itch,' Nancy said. 'A lot of men get it just because they think it's expected of them. We poor spinsters keep reading about such things just so that we'll be ready for marriage, if it ever comes. It'll pass though, it usually does.' Rose looked at her in disbelief. Really, Nancy was as thick as the wall. It wasn't Denis who had a seven-year itch. It was Rose. She was thirty-two years of age and, for the foreseeable future, her life was going to be exactly the same as it was now. A lifetime of smiling and covering her emotions had made Rose very circumspect. She was above all practical. There was no point in having a silly row with her friend and colleague Nancy.

'Maybe you're right, let's hope that's all it is,' she said, with her mind a million miles away from the mild expression on her face. Because Rose now realised the truth. She was restless and unsettled. She was looking for something, a little spark, a little dalliance. Possibly even a little affair. She felt a shiver of excitement and disbelief. She wasn't that kind of person. She had always thought wives who strayed were extraordinarily foolish. They deserved all they got, which was usually a very hard time. Rose found that, in the days that followed, everything had become even more same than it used to be. Denis said, 'Sorry, what was that?' to almost every single sentence she spoke to him, sometimes not waiting until she had finished. Maria Pilar every day said, 'I mess the buzz, the buzz was late.' It was useless to tell the stupid girl that either she was late or the bus was early. Rose gave up trying. Andrew said every day that he hated cornflakes and Celia, to copy him, said the same thing. Rose's mother phoned from Cork regularly to say how good the life was down there, how dignified, gracious and stylish compared to the brashness, vulgarity and violence of Dublin. Rose listened and murmured as she felt she had been doing for years. A meaningless murmur.

And then it was Sunday again. She prepared a rice salad 45

with black olives and pine nuts for the gathering at Ted and Susie's. She knew before they even rang at the door what Susie would say. Susie, a colourless woman, who would have looked very well if she had dyed her eyelashes and worn bright colours, in fact did say exactly as Rose had known: 'How clever you are. Rose. You always think of marvellous things. I don't know how you do it.'

Rose had the urge to scream at her that occasionally she opened a bloody cookbook, but stifled it. It would not be practical to shout at a friend, a hostess. She smiled and said it was nothing. She went into the room – there they all were, each playing the role that could have been written for them.

Bill was talking about the match, Gerry about the cost of airfares, her Denis was nodding sagely about Business Expansion Schemes, Nick was telling them about a horse he knew. And the women had roles too. Annie talked about the litter on the streets, Nessa about the rudeness of the people in the supermarket . . . Susie, as she always did, apologising and hoping everything was all right.

Rose's mind was a million miles away when Ted, standing beside her and spooning some of the rice salad on to his plate, said into her ear: 'Very exotic.' 'Oh it's quite simple really,' she began mechanically. 'I didn't mean the rice, I meant you.' he said, looking straight at her. Ted. Ted with the new car every year and the fairly vague job description, married to mousey Susie who had the money. 46 'Me?' Rose said, looking at him with interest. 'Well, your perfume, it's very exotic indeed. I always fancy that if we were all in the dark I'd find you immediately.' 'Well it's hard to prove, seeing that it's broad daylight,' she laughed with him, her eyes dancing like his. 'But it won't be daylight on Tuesday,' he said. 'Not in the night time, that is.' 'Now *what* made you make a deduction like that?' She was still playful but didn't sound puzzled or outraged. It was as if she were giving him permission and encouragement to go on. 'I'm going to Cork on business . . . overnight . . . and I thought that perhaps we could test out this theory of the perfume, you know. See whether I knew what part of the room you were in. What do you think?'

It was the moment to ask did he mean to include anyone else. It didn't need to be asked. 'And have you thought out how this could be managed?' she asked. She spoke in her ordinary voice as if they were talking about any of the same things they talked about in each other's houses for the last seven years. 'I gave it a load of thought,' said Ted, 'like it's your half term and you could be staying with your mother, as it were.' He was leaning on a shelf and looking at her. Interested. That's what he looked. It was a lovely, almost forgotten, feeling to have someone looking at her like that. Rose felt a tightening of her throat, a small lurch in her stomach. 'You've thought of everything,' she said. 'I don't see any obstacles, do you?' Ted might have been talking about garden furniture. 'Only the messy one of upsetting people,' she said. 'Ah, but you and I wouldn't do anything   47 like that. It's not as if we're falling in love or leaving anyone or breaking up any happy homes. It's just a bit of . . . well, how would I describe it . . . ?' 'A bit of excitement?' Rose suggested. 'Precisely,' he said.

She thought it was very sophisticated of them indeed not to make any plans and think up any cover stories. If it was going to happen, which she thought deep down it would, then these would all come later. They rejoined the group.

Rose let her glance fall over the others. Nessa and Susie and Annie, Grace. Did none of them ever ache for a little excitement in their lives? And if they did, who would they have found it with? Hardly her own Denis. He had barely time and energy for that kind of activity in his own house without thinking of arranging it with someone else's wife. The Sunday ended as every Sunday did with a visit to the pub. They had their traditions in this too. No big rounds meaning that people stayed all night. Each family bought their own drink. It was very civilised, like everything they did. And very, very dull, Rose realised.

As they left the pub for the car Andrew said he hated fizzy orange, and Celia, who had drunk very little other than fizzy orange in her life, said she hated it too. Denis opened the door of the car for Rose. 'Don't we have marvellous friends?' he said unexpectedly. 'We're very, very lucky.' She felt a hard knot of guilt form in her chest. But she swallowed it and agreed. 'But we work at it, of course,' Denis said. 'Having friends means a commitment of time and effort.'

Rose looked out the window. If working to achieve a Sunday exactly like this every single week was the result of time and commitment, then she was absolutely within her rights to want a day off, a night out. The knot of guilt had quite disappeared. Ted rang casually and told her there was a great place to leave her car in for an overhaul, only a few miles beyond Newlands Cross. Rose took down the details and thanked him. If the call had been bugged by every private detective and secret service in the world, it would have seemed totally innocent. Rose went into town and bought herself a black lace nightdress, a bottle of full-strength perfume with matching talcum powder and body lotion. If she was going to have a bit of excitement with Susie's handsome husband, he was going to remember it for a long time.

'I want to go to the zoo tomorrow,' Celia said at supper. 'That sounds nice,' said Denis, not looking up. 'Mummy's on half term.'

Rose looked at her son, hoping he would speak on cue. He did. 'I hate the zoo,' Andrew said. 'I hate the zoo too,' said Celia. 'That's settled then. Maria Pilar will take you out for a lovely walk and an ice-cream.' 'I get tired when I go on a lovely walk,' said Andrew. 'So, you can go on the buzz. Maria Pilar loves the buzz.' 'Eet is not the buzz, eet's the bussss,' said Maria Pilar, hissing across the table. 'So it is, I keep forgetting.' Rose got up briskly from the supper table. 'Now I've got lots to do, I'm off to see Grannie tomorrow.'

'I want to see Grannie,' Celia said. 'I hate Grannie,' Andrew said. Before Celia remembered that she hated Grannie also, Rose said no, this was a flying visit. 'Are you taking the plane?' Andrew asked with interest. His hatred of his grandmother might be tempered by a new experience like going in an aeroplane. 'Sorry what was that, you're going to see the old bat?' Denis asked.

'Has Grannie got a bat?' Andrew was very interested now. 'I want to see the bat,' Celia said. Rose glared at her husband. Now she would have to pretend that Grannie did have a bat. 'It's out a lot,' she said. 'Especially at night.' 'It's too much down and back in one day,' Denis said. 'I know, I'll stay the night.' Rose was surprised how easy it came when it had to, the lie, the cover-up. She always thought that women who weren't used to this would bluster or redden and give themselves away.

'You're doing your purgatory on earth, that's all I can say.' Denis left the supper table, and went into what they called his Denis' Den. He would be there until midnight. There were a lot of figures to be sorted out, coming up to sales conference time, he would tell her if she protested. Or Annual Report time or the AGM or the Visiting Firemen. There was always something.

Rose slept a guilt-free sleep. No woman was meant to sign on for such a dull life. That had been part of no bargain. Somewhere in the air there was a little clause allowing for a few Excitements along the way.

Ted was waiting exactly where he had said at ten o'clock. He was relaxed and easy. They transferred Rose's little overnight bag into his boot. 'This is great fun,' he said. 'Isn't it just?' said Rose. On the journey, they flirted with each other mildly. Rose said he drove the car in such a masterful way. Ted said she curled up like a kitten in a very seductive way. They played Chris de Burgh tapes. Ted had to do a few calls, but he had booked a table for lunch somewhere he thought Rose would like. Perhaps she'd like to settle into the hotel first and meet him at the restaurant. They didn't mention Denis or Susie. They told each other none of the cute little things said by Andrew and Celia or by Ted and Susie's children. This was an Excitement, time out and away from all that.

Rose examined the bedroom with approval . . . She hung up her good dress, hid all the perfumed unguents in her case. She didn't want it to look as if everything had come out of a bottle. She looked at her own face in the mirror. She was exactly the same as she had been last Sunday morning, only two days ago, before Ted had come up with the offer of the Excitement. The same, but a little more carefully groomed. She had waxed her legs. Always a dead give-away about affairs, people said, but Denis wouldn't have noticed. She strolled happily along to the restaurant where she was greeted by a cry that froze her blood. 'Rose, Rose, over here.' It was her mother.

Sitting with Nora Ryan, the most horrible person in the

South of Ireland or maybe in the whole of Ireland. A woman with beady eyes and a tongue that shot in and out like a snake's tongue, delivering harsh critical words every time. They were sitting at a table for three and they pulled out the third chair for her. Rose felt a pounding in her head. It was if they had expected her. 'How did you know I was . . . um . . . coming to see you . . . ?' she stammered. 'Well I rang. I rang and that not very bright girl said you were in zee Cork.' 'Europeans,' said Nora Ryan, casting her eyes up to heaven. 'We're all Europeans,' snapped Rose before she could stop herself. 'How observant of you, Rose dear,' said Nora Ryan with three flashes of her thin serpentine tongue.

'And what did you say?' Rose spoke to her mother. 'I said that's great, and that Nora and I were having lunch here but that stupid girl couldn't understand a word I said.' 'Spaniards!' said Nora, her eyes nearly reaching the brim of her hideous hat. 'So what did you do then?' Rose felt a sense of blind panic that she had never known before.

Now the unthinkable had happened. Her mother must have told her husband there had never been any question of a visit. Was there a hope in hell Rose could pretend it had been meant as a surprise? 'I had a very odd conversation with my grandson who seemed to think the house was infested with bats and that you were coming down to deal with them.' Rose put her head in her hands. 'So then obviously I rang Denis at the office to find out what was happening.' 'And what did he say?' 'Questions, questions, really Rose, you're like one of these interrogators on television,' said Nora Ryan. Rose flashed her a look of pure loathing. 'Mother, what did Denis say?'

'He said he was well, he said he was busy coming up to the Sales Conference . . .' 'Before I have to take you by the throat and beat it out of you, Mother, what did he say about my coming to Cork? What did he say?' 'Really, Rose,' Nora Ryan began. 'Shut up, Mrs Ryan,' said Rose.

They stared at her. Rose tried to recover the lost ground. She spoke very slowly, as if talking to someone of a very low IQ. 'Can-I-ask-you-Mother-to-tell-me-what-did-Denis say?' Rose's mother was fingering her throat, the one that Rose had threatened to shake her by. She seemed almost afraid to speak. 'I don't see *why* you're talking like this Rose, I really don't. I told Denis that if you called before you went out to the house this is where we'd be having lunch. To save you . . . to *save* you the journey out to the house . . . that's what I was doing and inviting you to lunch in a nice smart place like this . . .' Rose's mother had taken out a handkerchief and dabbed the corner of her eye. 'I most certainly didn't expect dogs' abuse and interrogation about it.' She was hurt and she didn't mind them knowing it. Mrs Ryan was now in the totally unaccustomed role of being a consoler. 'Now now, now now now,' she said, patting the shaking shoulder awkwardly and flashing glances of hate at Rose. 'Did he know I was coming to stay with you?' Rose's voice was dangerously calm, the words came out with long spaces between them.

'Of course he knew,' her mother sniffled. 'How did he know?' 'I told him.' 'How did *you* know, Mother?' Rose's mother and Nora Ryan looked at each other in alarm. Perhaps Rose was going mad . . . seriously mad. 'Because Maria Pilar had told me, my grandchildren had told me . . .' The breath seemed to come out of Rose more easily now. 'Yes. Well that's fine, that's all cleared up,' she said. And at that moment Ted came into the room, carrying a single red rose wrapped in cellophane. The blood drained from her head yet again.

He saw her and came over. 'What a surprise. What a huge surprise,' he shouted like a very bad actor in an amateur play. The two older women looked at each other again, their alarm increased. 'Good God . . . it's Ted,' cried Rose. 'Of *all* the people in the world!' She looked around the room as if she expected to see a few other equally unexpected people, like Napoleon or Princess Diana. 'I'll tell you the most extraordinary thing,' Ted shouted, unaware that the entire dining room was now looking at them and could not avoid listening to them. 'This is my mother,' screamed Rose. 'My mother that I was coming down to Cork to visit.' 'How do you do?' Rose's mother began, but she might as well have been talking to the wall.

'The *most* extraordinary thing,' Ted repeated. 'I was back at the hotel before . . . um . . . before coming along here and who did I meet but Susie's brother and his wife.

Susie is my wife,' he said to the sixty or so people who were now part of his listenership. 'They are in Cork and staying in the same hotel.' He paused to let the words sink in with all the diners. 'The very same hotel.' He didn't get the reaction he wanted, whatever it might have been, so he said it in a different form. 'The *self-same* hotel, I think you might say,' he said triumphantly.

Rose began to babble. 'That's lovely for you Ted, you can all be together. I'd love to stay in a hotel myself sometime, but I'm staying with my *mother*.' Mrs Ryan looked at her with narrowed eyes. 'I'm sure your mother wouldn't mind at all if you were to stay in a hotel,' she said pleasantly. 'No, no, no, I can't. And anyway, Mother has a lot of bats in the house,' she floundered wildly to Ted, 'so that's where I'll be staying.' Ted might not even have heard her.

'So the odd thing was that when they thought they saw me, they asked at Reception was that me and Reception of course, God damn interfering nosey parkers that they are, said that Mr *and* Mrs Ted O'Connor were there.' Rose said, 'What did you do?' 'I told them that suddenly at the last moment Susie couldn't come and then Reception said did I want to move to a single room because it woud be cheaper and I said yes, but that I'd rush up and pack my things and so I did and they're in the back of the car, if you know what I mean.'

Rose looked at him. His face was scarlet, he looked like a madman talking to other very mad people. 'If you get my drift,' he roared. Rose felt a sudden maturity sweep over her. She knew now that she had enough excitement to last her a long time. On the grounds that she was helping Ted to park his car, she left with him, retrieved her suitcase. They were both too shocked to speak. She returned to the restaurant where the diners looked up with interest, hoping for Round Two. Ted had given the red rose to Mrs Ryan. 'I bought it for you,' he had said without explanation. Nora Ryan saw nothing odd in this. In her youth it had happened a lot, she said. Rose spoke courteously to her mother, planned the night in the house that she had forgotten was bat-free and worked out what train to get back to Dublin and how to retrieve her car from beyond Newlands Cross. To begin what she hoped would be a fairly even-tempered and unexciting period of her life.

A Note on Maeve Binchy

Maeve Binchy was born in Co Dublin and went to school at Holy Child Convent in Killiney. She took a history degree at UCD and taught at various girls' schools, writing travel articles in the long summer holidays. In 1969 she joined the *Irish Times*, and has written humorous columns from London and all over the world. The Peacock Theatre in Dublin was the scene of her two stage plays, *End of Term* and *Half Promised Land*, and her television play, *Deeply Regretted By*, won two Jacobs Awards and the Best Script Award at the Prague Film Festival. Her last four novels, including *The Copper Beech* and *The Glass Lake*, were number one bestsellers and her books have been adapted for television and cinema, most notably *Circle of Friends* which was one of the most successful films in 1995. Her new novel, *Evening Class*, will be published by Orion in 1996. She is married to the writer and broadcaster Gordon Snell.

Other titles in this series